The Travelling Pillow

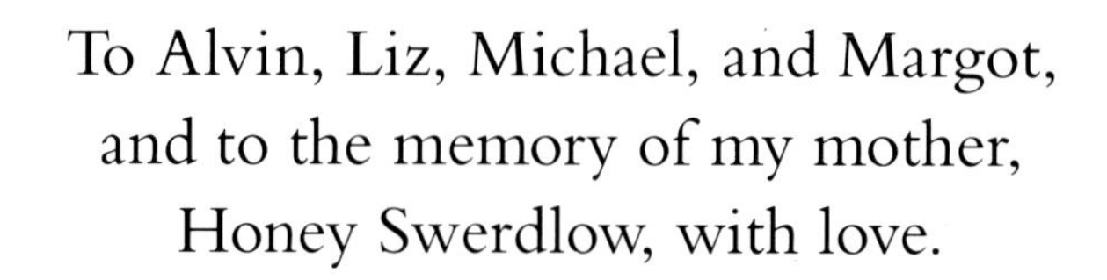

To Alvin, Liz, Michael, and Margot,
and to the memory of my mother,
Honey Swerdlow, with love.

Typography by Alicia Mikles
Published by Greene Bark Press Inc.,
PO Box 1108
Bridgeport, CT 06601-1108

Library of Congress Catalog # 94-75990
Library of Congress Cataloging in Publication Data
Brown, Beverly Swerdlow
The Story of the Traveling Pillow

Summary: The tale of a pillow originally sewn as
a gift by Panda for her friend Mouse and the long
series of events which follow as the pillow is
passed from one owner to another.
1. Children's Stories, American. [1. Pillow-Fiction]
1. Ott, Margot J., ill 11. Title

Printed in Hong Kong
ISBN# 1-88085 1-12-1

The TRAVELLING PILLOW

By Beverly Swerdlow Brown
Illustrated by Margot Janet Ott

GREENE BARK PRESS, INC.
P.O. Box 1108
Bridgeport, CT 06601-1108

Panda looked in the closets. Then she looked in some drawers. Finally she found what she was looking for: scraps of material and yarn.

“I’m going to make a pillow!” she said, and happily began to sew.

Three days later Panda was done. “This is a terrific pillow!” she said. “But what should I do with it?” She thought and thought.

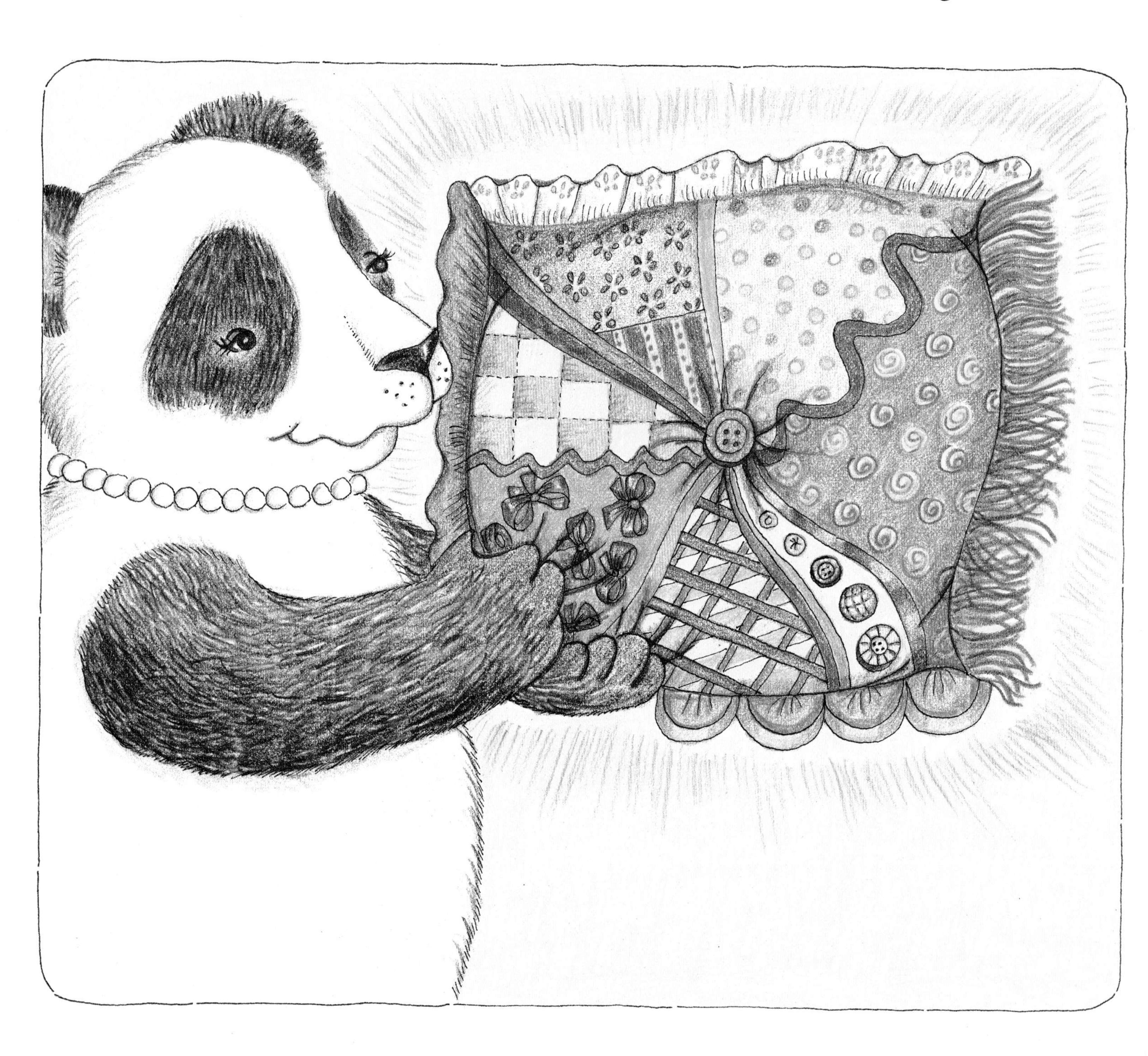

"I'll give the pillow to Mouse," said Panda. "She collects them!" Panda rode on a bus to Mouse's house.

“Here is a pillow I made,” said Panda. “I thought that you might like it!” “Thank you.” said Mouse, raising her eyebrow at the strange-looking cushion. “It’s really different!” Panda smiled and went home,

"Now," said Mouse, "if only I can think of somewhere to put it!" She looked around and put the pillow on a rocker. "No, that doesn't look right," she said.

Then she put the pillow on a footstool
"No, that doesn't look right either."

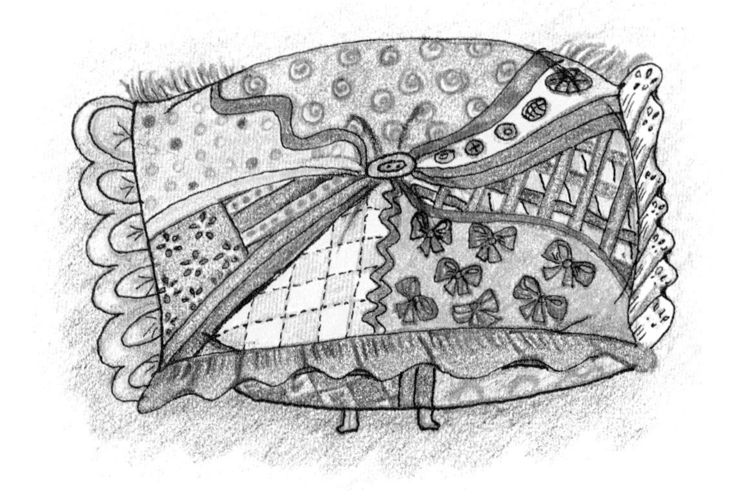

So she put the pillow on the floor.
"No, that doesn't look right at all,"
she sighed. "What should I do with it?"

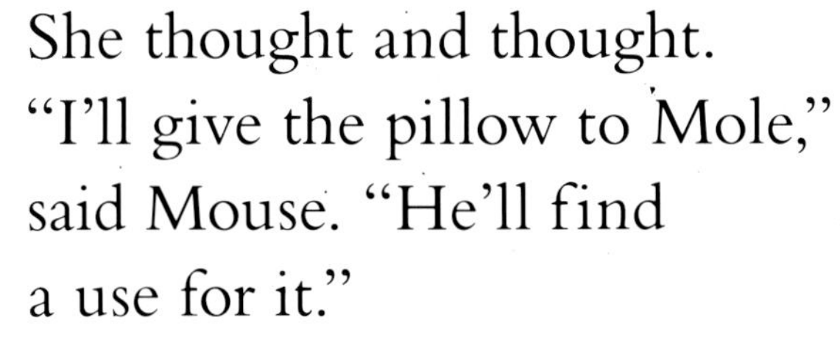

She thought and thought.
"I'll give the pillow to Mole,"
said Mouse. "He'll find
a use for it."

Mouse went over to her neighbor's yard. "Here is a wonderful pillow for you," she said.

“Gee thanks, said Mole, squinting and sniffing at it. Mouse smiled and went home.

“Mmmmmmm,” thought Mole, dragging the pillow back to his burrow. “This will make a scrumptious bed!”

But, no matter how hard he poked, or squeezed, or pushed, the pillow just would not fit through his door. "Oh dear," he sighed. "Now what should I do with it?"

He thought and thought. "I'm having a yard sale tomorrow," he said. "I'm sure someone will buy it!"

The next day, Mole put the pillow out in front of his yard with his other things.

A little while later, Giraffe drove by.
When he saw the pillow, he said,
“That is magnificent!” It belongs
in my museum!”

Giraffe paid Mole, picked up the pillow, and drove away.

"Where should I put this?" he thought, walking through the museum. He looked all around and put the pillow on a pedestal. "No, that's not right," he said.

Then he put the pillow in a glass case."No, that's not right either."

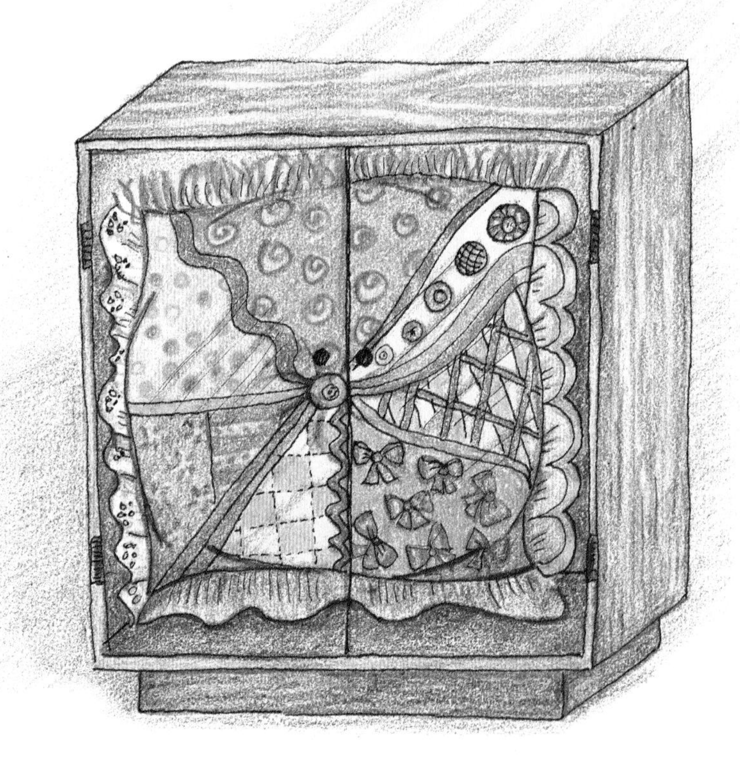

So he hung the pillow up on a wall, where only he could see it. “Ah, yes,” he sighed. “That’s just right!”

While Giraffe was admiring the pillow, Crow flew by the window and peeked in. She grinned. "I must have that pillow!" she thought."It will make a fabulous nest!"

Just then, Giraffe's phone rang. When he went to answer it, Crow flew into the museum, plucked the pillow off the wall, and flew out of the window with it.

"Criminy!" cried Crow, flying lower and lower. "This thing is really heavy!"

First she tried to hold the pillow with her feet, but that didn't work.

Then she tried to grasp the pillow in her beak, but that didn't work either.

And when she tried to balance it on her back, that didn't work at all.

The pillow slipped off . . . and dropped right in front of Pig, who was on his way to the park.

"What a neat pillow!" he said, surprised. He picked it up and hugged it to his chest. "It's so nice and soft," he said.

Then he juggled it on his nose. "It's so light and bouncy, too!"

Next he tossed the pillow into the air and when it came down, it landed on his head. "This is fun!" he laughed.

Crow grumbled as she hovered over Pig. "Oh well . . . he can have that dumb old pillow for all I care!" And away she flew, while Pig skipped merrily along.

He was having such a good time, he didn't see Elephant and bumped smack into him. Elephant caught his breath. "My," he said "but that's a marvelous pillow you're wearing!"

Thank you, said Pig smiling. “I think your straw hat is pretty nifty, too!” “Really?” said Elephant. “Then would you be willing to trade your pillow for my hat?” Pig thought and thought. “Why not,” he said, and each got what he wanted. Then Pig skipped off, while Elephant trotted across town to his office.

By the time he got there, he was so tired he could hardly keep his eyes open. “Now, where can I put this pillow?”he yawned. Sleepily he pressed the pillow to the file cabinet, but when he leaned against it, the pillow squished, “Gosh, he sighed. “This won’t do!”

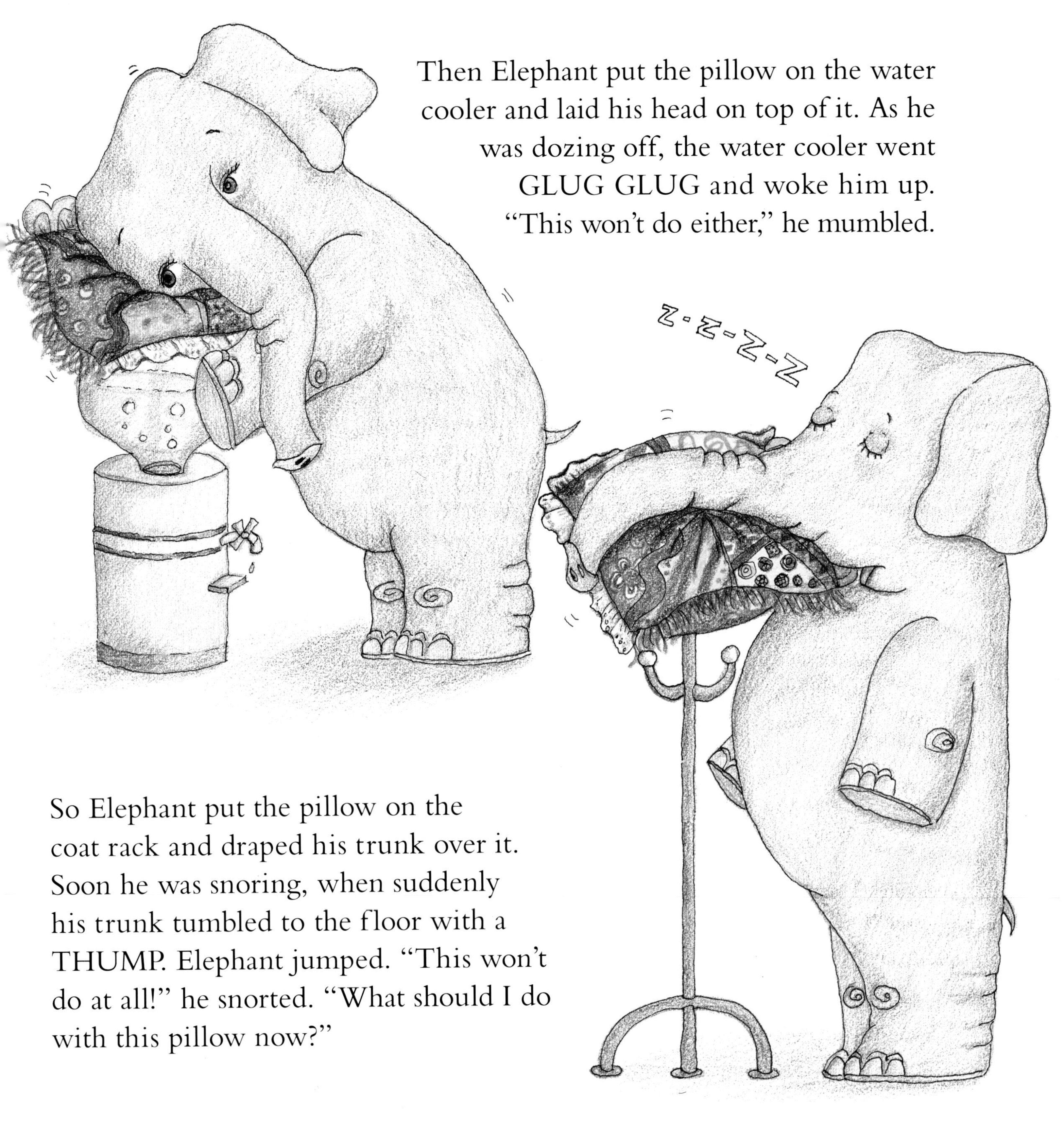

Then Elephant put the pillow on the water cooler and laid his head on top of it. As he was dozing off, the water cooler went GLUG GLUG and woke him up. "This won't do either," he mumbled.

So Elephant put the pillow on the coat rack and draped his trunk over it. Soon he was snoring, when suddenly his trunk tumbled to the floor with a THUMP. Elephant jumped. "This won't do at all!" he snorted. "What should I do with this pillow now?"

He thought and thought. "I know, he said. "I'll give the pillow to my sister. She sells one-of-a-kind things in her store!"

The next day, Elephant brought the pillow to her. “Thanks!” said his sister. “I sure don’t have any thing like this!”

That afternoon, Panda passed by the store. Something caught her eye. She looked in the window. “My word,” she gasped. “A pillow just like the one I made! I’ll buy it and give it to Mouse! Then she will have two pillows exactly alike!”